Hit and Run

Upstate Mystery, Volume 1

ɧ donohue

Published by ɧ donohue, 2021.

HIT AND RUN

First edition. May 21, 2021.

Copyright © 2021 ʄ donohue.

ISBN: 979-8215674161

Written by ʄ donohue.

HIT AND RUN
AN UPSTATE COZY MYSTERY
BY FJ DONOHUE

With grateful thanks to my good friend
Thomas E Burch
For his technical help,
And to my wife
Louise
For her editing

Prologue

THE SEASONS WERE CHANGING. Fall had not quite arrived but now the nights were clear and the summer heat long gone. The driver of the car was on his way home after having dinner and watching a movie at his soon to be wife's house. On the way home his car started to run rough and then the engine quit. It was not a lack of fuel as he had almost three-quarters of a tank of gas. Could be electrical but the lights, radio and navigation system were still working. He pulled the car over on the shoulder of the two-lane county road to see what he could do. He got some tools from the trunk and opened the hood to look around. No odor indicating an electrical or oil leak issue, just a funny sort of sweet smell from around the engine. He tried repeatedly to start the car but it only drained the battery. He would need to get the car towed to a repair shop. He called his local guy on his mobile phone and waited.

He was outside the car waiting when an oncoming vehicle slowed down a bit and flashed its high beams. He stepped out from the hard shoulder and waved his hands to make sure the driver saw him and the car. The oncoming car put on its right signal indicator showing he was pulling over. Standing near the middle of his car he waved at the driver. The driver slowed the car to about 30mph and then at around 60 feet from the disabled car with the driver standing next to it, he accelerated rapidly and struck both car and driver. The victim never had a chance. He tried to run to the front of the car but only got as far as the left front fender. The victim was smashed against the side of his car and killed instantly. He ended up 20 feet in front of his disabled car.

Chapter 1

SHIT-OH-DEAR, HE WAS glad that was over.

You never know how a mediation will turn out. The parties in a mediation may genuinely want to reach an agreement or they may spend all their time pissing on each other's shoes. This one had a definite urine component, a strong one! The parties in this mediation were in the process of divorcing and were attempting to sort out their responsibilities regarding their children. The court had sent them to the Resolution Center where Brad volunteered. The mediation process would allow them to sort matters out for themselves rather than have an overworked judge decide their future.

Custody, visitation, primary residence. It either goes well or is a dog fight. Brad knew he had a problem when they referred to the children as "my children", not "our children." Long sessions ahead he thought. He usually worked with the parties in two-hour blocks as history told him that after that, the fatigue factor set in and any progress could even go negative. After three two-hour sessions the parties, John, aka Jake and Linda had finally arrived at an agreement. An agreement? Well, that is what the court order would say, but Brad knew it would not work. With all the holidays split down to the arrival and departure time on each of the days, it was bound to crash and burn but for now, take the money and run. They could always come back and modify it as required and maybe, in time, they would.

Anyway, it was over - for now!

Chapter 2

BRAD WAS RETIRED FROM the District Attorney's office in upstate New York. He had been an investigator. His job had been to review pending cases to provide an input and guidance on the crime in question. Did they have sufficient evidence? Would it survive a Grand Jury hearing? Was it solid? If so, send it forward. If not, do some more digging. Don't go in front of the Grand Jury without all your ducks in a row.

Before working at the DA's office, he had been a police detective and had been badly wounded while apprehending a fugitive who had murdered one of his colleagues. After that, front-line police work was not really an option. The investigator job with the DA allowed him to do the work he loved in a less hostile environment. His work had been more of a desk job. If an arrest was required, the police were called. The nature of the work had suited him and he enjoyed the complexity of it. Let the evidence show the path forward.

Although there was not a mandatory retirement age with the county DA, he had finally reached a point where he felt it was time to make the big adjustment - retire and move on. Long winters in Tampa, then back in Broome County doing mediations at the Resolution Center. And working on a mediocre golf game soon became part of his lifestyle in both places. He had trained to become a mediator, and handling cases made for busy days. Even after his years of investigative work, mediation turned out to be a real eye opener. The goal is to help the parties reach decisions regarding their life and the children's life outside of Family Court. The courts were always very busy with cases and they worked with the Resolution Center to allow the parties to reach their own decisions and not have the courts mandate their outcomes. Like many things in life, some are easy and some are far from it. This last case tested the limits: 6 hours. The couple entered the meeting room fighting and left fighting. But they did have an agreement in place and at least something to build on if they can could look ahead and not back. We shall see, thought Brad.

Brad and his wife Lulu, who he often called Queenie, still lived in a small house. They had downsized after the kids were gone and it fit them. They had a good network of friends and this was their home. His wife had decorated it so nicely and it all fit. Lulu had retired from teaching French language and literature at the university, then she had taken on a new career writing romance novels and children's books. His life was structured to make sure the days were full and active: mornings at the Jewish Community Center (JCC) doing Pilates and kettlebell exercises, mediations involving parenting issues or small claims at the Resolution Center downtown. Also golf and going for walks with man's best friend, Tasha. She was half Husky and Sheppard. A rescue dog eight years ago and now the ruler of the house, always happy to see him and listen to his stories. Two of their children who lived in the Boston area kept on at them to move closer but for now, things were working well. So, put off that decision for another day.

Chapter 3

WHY IS IT SO HARD TO hit a golf shot on a fairway with a downslope? Be careful or you will hit it fat. And he did, yet again. You would think that after playing golf for all these years, he would have worked it out but yet there it was again: chunk, chunk, chunk. He was playing on one of his favorite local courses with his golf partners. The course was a local public course. Its main attraction was that it was a "Billy Goat" course. Out in the country on probably an old farm with lots of hills. Level shots were not the norm. At least the greens were honest and well maintained. They all played at the same skill level and frankly, nobody cared what the other guy scored. He had long passed playing for money so it was always a nice relaxed atmosphere. Play your game. He was on the 16th hole. A longish 140-yard par three. Water on both sides. Time to be fearless!

His shot was not too bad, about 10 yards short of the green, but dry. Life is good!

He had not heard from Spud in a while and was surprised to see his name on the caller ID. Andy Prono, AKA, Spud was an investigator for the DA. He and Brad had worked together before Brad retired.

"Am I speaking to the famous B-Rad"?

"You are Spud, do I owe you any money?"

"Nothing that easy, do you have some time to talk?"

"I'm on the golf course and almost finished. Can I call you back when I get to the clubhouse? Should be about 20-30 minutes".

"Sure, how're you playing?"

"What's your next question?"

"Oops, sorry, talk to you shortly."

Bogey, bogey, bogey on 16,17,18. Not a bad finish. He usually got into trouble on at least two of the final three holes. He returned Spud's call on the number he had used to call him and noticed that it was his office number. So, maybe not a social call. Spud picked up on the second ring.

"So, what can I do for you?"

"Brad, do you remember the accident out on Colesville road about 2 months ago? Guy was killed by a hit and run while trying to sort out a car problem on the side of the road".

"Sure do, read about it in the papers and it also made the local TV news."

"Well, in running through all the paperwork on the case, I saw that the dead guy was divorced and he and his ex-wife had been clients at the Resolution Center. Do you still do work there? I would like to talk to the mediator on the case if you can arrange it. We're not comfortable with some recent findings."

"Speaking!"

"What! You were the mediator?"

"Yes, it was a long session and they were not happy campers. There were a lot of bad feelings between them. The guy was in the process of marrying his new girlfriend so there was even more animosity between them. She accused him of infidelity during their marriage".

"Did you get the impression he had cheated during the marriage?" Spud asked.

"Hard to say and when you are doing a mediation, you try to keep them focused on the future, not the past."

"Ok, I get that, but was there anything unusual about the mediation that you recall?"

"Well as I said there were a lot of bad feelings between them. However, I do remember one comment she made when he said he would shortly marry again."

"What did she say?"

"Well it was odd that she spoke with such conviction. *She said that will never happen.* I wondered at the time if she had some information about him which she would make public or disclose to his new lady. Usually the other party is hurt when their ex remarries but this seemed to be a lot more than that."

"Do you have any notes from the mediation?" asked Spud.

"Not really. We don't keep our notes at the conclusion. What you have from Family Court is essentially what would be on file at the office."

"OK, what you've remembered is interesting and sort of confirms my thinking. Let me review this with the DA. Can I call you back on this?"

"Sure, keep in touch."

Chapter 4

SPUD FOUND MARY LOUISE Eldridge in her office. For once, she had a minute to spare. She had been the DA for 7 years now. She was popular and had a good reputation. The office in the past had been used as a stepping stone to higher offices and as such had suffered from heavy-handed politics. When Mary Louise, then an Assistant District Attorney, decided to run for DA, she was not given much of a chance. However, during the campaign she showed that she was competent and committed to the office. Her good looks and athletic dancer's build served her well also. She won decidedly and the good old boys had to find another avenue for career progression.

"OK Spud, what do you want?"

"Well you had asked me to take another look at the hit and run on Colesville road based on the information we obtained from the junkyard.

"I did and was there anything new?"

"Not conclusive but there is an odor here that does not seem to go away".

"Meaning?"

"Brad Petronella is a volunteer mediator at the Resolution Center and as it turns out he was the mediator when the court sent the parties over there to sort out the parenting issues with the children.

"I heard that Brad was volunteering there, how's he doing?"

"Good, we still meet up for lunch or drinks at the Ale House. I think he is quite happy in his new life."

"Glad to hear it, he was one of the best detective/investigators I have ever worked with. I remember when he was a lead detective with the police department and I was a lowly assistant DA. His case material was always solid and backed up. I never got caught short trying his cases."

"For sure. He guided me through the learning curve" agreed Spud.

"I miss him," said Mary Louise, "fun to be around and a great investigator".

"That's what bothers me now," replied Spud.

"What d'you mean?"

"Brad always was a dogged investigator but more than that he has great intuition. He sees things, feels things that the rest of us might not pick up on. Running with his intuition, he would dig a bit deeper and before you know it, new facts, new life to the case, and a solution. I've seen it over and over. I wish I had his nose for that."

"You do okay, Spud. We trust and rely on you".

"Thanks, if I can see the spear in the guy's chest, I can usually sort out the cause of death!"

Mary Louise laughed. Then she said seriously, "So summarize where we are with this crime of the century."

"Well, we know Jake Hagan was killed by a hit and run driver on the side of the Colesville road," said Spud. "The hood and trunk of his car were open and tools were found on the road. It appears that he was attempting to fix his car. We never found the hit and run driver or his car. That vehicle must have been significantly damaged, based on the condition of Hagan's car, but he or she did manage to drive away. No vehicle was ever recovered. The cops did a paint analysis from the crash site and determined that the vehicle was a white Toyota. It's a common color used by Toyota for years on many of their models. Still in use today. We checked the body shops and salvage yards around Broome and surrounding counties and didn't find any recent work done on a white Toyota".

Mary Louise said, "OK, no leads. What happened next?"

"The cops sent the victim's car to Downs Salvage Yard after they were finished with it. Linda Hagan told them to scrap it out as it was badly damaged and probably could not be repaired. This is when it gets interesting. When the yard man at Downs drained the fluids from the car before they put it in the yard, the guy found that the gas tank was loaded with sugar!"

"Really?" Mary Louise said. "Does this mean that the engine would stop?"

"More than stop," said Spud. "It would be destroyed".

"So what does this have to do with the hit and run?"

"Jake Hagan was with his future wife at her place on Court St. Apparently from there he was headed back to his home on Colesville road."

"OK that's nice, but what's the issue here?"

"I asked the yard guy at Gary's how far a car could go with a load of sugar in the tank. He said assuming it was not in the tank for days and the gas in the tank was not compromised, the car could go as far as the uncontaminated gas in the line allowed, and maybe a bit further. If the sugar was there long enough to be absorbed into the gas throughout, that would be another story."

"Okay," said Mary Louise. "How far?"

"Depends on the car but we think between 5 and 10 miles."

"Hmm." Mary Louise thought about it. "When Jake left his girlfriend's house on Court St it was a quick turn onto Colesville road and then a straight shot to his house. So it was likely that the car would fail along the road to his house?"

Spud said, "I think so, it fits. I met with the police regarding this, but as you can see, nothing conclusive: no hit and run car found and the victim's car was processed at Downs salvage yard. They looked into it but not much they could do with the lack of evidence. A couple of kids could have spiked the gas tank. Who knows?"

"Okay," said Mary Louise, "what brings Brad into this?"

"I called Brad as I noticed when I was reviewing the file that the Hagans had gone through a parenting mediation at the Resolution

Center. I wondered what thoughts the mediators might have about the couple. How did they behave during the sessions, that sort of thing?"

"And?" Mary Louise said.

"It was a dog fight. Took three sessions to sort out the parenting issues and guess who the mediator was?"

"Don't tell me," said Mary Louise, "B-Rad?"

Spud replied, "Oh yes, and don't let him hear you calling him that or he will go back to calling you Boss Lady!"

"Good point, thanks," Mary Louise replied. "Tell me about Brad's spin on this."

"When I asked him about the case, he remembered it quite well as it was long and difficult. I asked if there was anything special that stood out in his mind and he said yes. Linda Hagan made an odd comment when it became apparent that Jake planned to remarry," replied Spud. *She said that will never happen.* It was said with such conviction that he thought she must have some real evidence for it. Social or monetary issues, maybe. He didn't know, but was left with a feeling that this was much more than an idle threat. If it had been any other mediator than Brad, I might not have placed too much stock in the comment. But you know Brad, he just has a feel for these things. So put it all together: hit and run and no car or driver recovered, sugar in the gas tank that would pretty much define the breakdown point and Brad's intuition, and you get an odor to this whole mess.

"OK Spud," said Mary Louise, "what do you want to do?"

"I've eight open cases on my desk now and this case will require a lot of time and research," replied Spud. "If we have something here, it will be hard to dig it out. So, I am wondering if we can bring Brad back on a limited basis and see what he can come up with. If anyone can make sense of this, he can."

"Call him," said his boss.

Chapter 5

BRAD WAS ON HIS WAY home to pick up his wife, LuLu. They were going out to dinner at a place of her choosing. He liked all kinds of cuisines so was never disappointed. However, his steak low level light was on and maybe they could go to Bud's in Apalachin. He had just finished a long walk in the woods with Tasha at a nearby nature preserve. Tasha was happy to be left alone in the evening to guard the fort from the comfort of her large cushion. His cell phone rang and he was glad for the Bluetooth hands-free connection. In earlier days, he had taken too many chances using the phone while driving. Spud came on the line.

"B-Rad, I am calling to offer some life altering advice."

"Oh joy, how much will it cost?"

"Nada my man but I would like to speak with you about the Hagan case and possible next steps"

"OK, when do you want to meet?"

"How about breakfast at The Park Diner tomorrow, 09:00 hours?"

"Can do, see you then."

Brad liked the Park Diner. Good coffee and sausages. It had been around for years and as you get older, the predictability of places seems to grow in importance.

Brad wondered what Spud had in mind. He had told him all he knew about the case from his role in the mediation sessions. Other than that he did not have anything more to bring to the table. Maybe Spud was looking for a sounding board.

At 9AM the diner wasn't crowded. The working crowd had departed and they easily found a quiet corner to talk.

"What's going on?" asked Brad. "I'm not sure I have anything more to add to our earlier conversation."

"Well let me lay out what we know and where we want to take this show."

Brad didn't know any details of the actual hit and run other than what had been on the news. The police report Brad showed him was graphic and frankly disturbing. He had investigated many hit and run accidents over the years, but this one was different. Spud then talked about the sugar in the gas tank, the range of the vehicle under those conditions, the distance between Jake's place and his girlfriend's house and their locations. He also briefed him on the police involvement. They were interested, but lacking hard evidence, were struggling to take it further.

"Brad, this case has an odor to it that won't go away. I don't want to make this sound like more than it is, but there are too many open ends."

"I agree, Spud, but where do you want to take it?"

"That's where you come in."

"Me? I'm out to pasture. I'm not a player anymore."

"True, but Mary Louise and I want to ask you to do some part-time work for us on the case. We don't have the manpower to put on it and the police have backed off. We need someone like you to dig into it and see where it takes you. We need some solid legwork to find out what we have. Neither the DA or I want to shut the case down yet. Take a look at it. Keep us posted on developments. We can meet periodically to assess the situation. If it does turn out to be a murder, the police will take over and the DA will call a Grand Jury and go to trial."

"Wow, this is a real gear change for me. I need to think about it. I don't want to start this and just tickle it for a few months. If I agree to do this, I need to take it to the end."

"After all these years, I wouldn't expect anything different from you. I'm not sure of the compensation, I guess you bill us hours. I need to check with Mary Louise and see how she wants to handle it."

"Not to worry, new cars and Hawaiian vacations will be fine!"

"When can you start?"

"I think I've already started emotionally, but check with her and if she still wants to do this, I can get right on it"

"How are you going to approach this?"

"I don't know. Right now it's a two-scotch problem. Let me sleep on it. Get me all the files so I can try to understand all the players. By the way, who was looking into this at the Police department?"

"Raimondi."

"Good, Phil is a steady hand."

Chapter 6

IT IS ALWAYS A CHALLENGE when you first start on a case. Where to begin? What is the scope of the enquiry? Who are the players? It can go on forever in terms of issues to understand. Brad always made a point of spending a lot of time reviewing the case files. All of them, files from the police, the coroner and the DA. At this point all the information has value and needs to be assessed. Nothing is trivial. Review the files, then review them again. And yes, do it once more. Brad always found some item he had missed. He needed to get his arms around the problem. From there the next steps would be logical. Get a plan, stay the course, don't get sidetracked. Easy to say, maybe not so easy to do.

So, who were the players? So far, not too many:

Jake and Linda Hagan
Jake's girlfriend and future spouse Carol
Linda's boyfriend, Bodie Varilly
Jake and Linda's children: Gary (11), Darlene (9) both from the marriage

What do we have for files?

Police report of the accident and subsequent investigation
DA's report
Divorce agreement
Autopsy report on Jake

Brad started with the police report on the hit and run. It happened between 1 and 2 AM on October 10th. There were no adverse weather-related conditions. The night was clear. The accident was called in on 911 from a passing motorist who stayed at the scene. He did not notice anything other than the hit and run. He stated that when he called 911, the Sheriff and EMS were on the scene within 15 minutes which was a timely response given the location. The motorist did not touch the wrecked car. He only checked the victim and it was obvious he was dead. The vehicle was impounded by the Sheriff and taken for analysis. The driver's side door and left front fender of the victim's car were substantially damaged. There was blood and paint deposits from the hit and run vehicle on the victim's car. The victim had been thrown approximately 20-feet in front of the vehicle and suffered massive injuries. He died instantly from the impact.

Other than the paint deposits on the victim's car from the hit and run vehicle, there was no other evidence such as parts or pieces from the hit and run vehicle that could help identify the make and model of the car. The only defining evidence was the paint marks on the victim's car. A subsequent analysis of the paint showed that it was an off-white color used by Toyota. It was a mainline color in production on a variety of Toyota models and still in use. So, all he knew was that the hit and run vehicle was a white Toyota. Model and year could not be determined.

As Spud had said earlier, a canvas of the body shops and salvage yards in the county and adjacent ones did not turn up any repairs on a white Toyota vehicle. A handwritten note at the end of the police report caught Brad's eye. When the police had finished their analysis of the car they called Linda Hagan about the disposition of the vehicle. Why Linda? They were divorced after all, why would she have any role in the disposition of the vehicle? Had she gotten the car in the divorce settlement? Didn't Jake keep it? The note in the file also said she told them to send the car to Downs's junkyard on Colesville Road to be scrapped. The note was dated November 9th. So, now the victim's car was long gone and not available for any further research. Curious though, that it was Linda who made the call on the disposition on the vehicle.

An addendum was also attached to the police report detailing the findings reported by the Downs yard man about the sugar in the gas tank. It was a brief statement only saying that it had been noticed while preparing the car to be put in the yard. As the vehicle was long gone, any chance of fingerprints around the gas cap or fender area was not possible. Too bad. Nothing in the file about any follow up investigation, so the case was for all practical purposes dormant. Brad would check with Phil Raimondi at police headquarters to check that this was the current status. The track appeared to be at an end except for Linda's role in the disposition of the vehicle.

Chapter 7

BRAD NEXT WENT TO THE divorce decree to see how the assets were to be distributed. As it turned out, there was not a lot to look at. The house was being sold, the money to be split between the parties. Jake Hagan did not have much interest in the contents of the house other than his tools, so they agreed he would get the tools and Linda Hagan would get the contents of the house. There were two cars in the settlement. The Nissan Altima went to Linda and the Chevy Equinox to Jake. But Jake was driving the Altima when he was killed. Why? Could be a simple answer or maybe something more. Make a note of it and run it down. Nothing more of interest in the decree. Child support was addressed, primary residence and joint custody as well was addressed. The decree directed that child visitation schedule be settled through mediation at the Resolution Center. Brad then called Spud at the DA's office and asked him to contact the DMV

and verify that the Nissan was registered to Linda Hagan. He was pretty sure there was no mistake, but needed to be sure.

Next up was the DA's report. It was essentially a follow-on of the police report. Nothing new in the file other than a bit more detail on the crash scene and the results of an interview with the yard man regarding the sugar in the gas tank. Of particular note was the question about when the sugar would have been put into the gas tank. According to the yard man and a third-party expert Spud used, they both agreed that it had to be the same night of the hit and run and most likely within a few hours of the car being used. If it had been earlier in the day, the whole fuel system would have been compromised and most likely, the engine would not have started or if it did, it would have failed within minutes. Spud had briefed Brad on this earlier. That would mean the hit and run was not only premeditated but carefully choreographed. Why? Why set it up for a hit and run? Or was it maybe just to get Jake stuck out on a deserted road late at night? Trying to time a hit and run using a compromised gas mixture seemed like a long shot to Brad. Stranding Jake out on the road with a broken car might be more realistic. Brad decided to sleep on it all and look at it again in the morning. Rule of thumb was always three careful reviews of the files and then plan the next steps.

Chapter 8

NEXT DAY, FRIDAY, BRAD was playing golf at En-Joie Golf club, a local public course that hosted the PGA Senior Tour. The course was always well maintained in anticipation of the Senior tour in the late summer and the local golfers were always respectful of the course.

This time, on the sixth hole Brad's cell phone rang. It was Spud. "Hey, B-Rad, have you solved the case yet?"

"I have, and just as I thought, the butler did it!"

"I always suspected him. Arrest that man!" said Spud.

Then Brad said, "I have some information for you from the DMV regarding the vehicle registrations."

"Great, what have you got?"

"Well, the Altima is registered to Linda and the Equinox to Jake."

"That's backwards, what's going on?"

"I don't really know. Doesn't make a lot of sense. Keep it on your "to do" list of things to sort out."

"Okay. Got to get back to the game, I am up next on the tee."

"Challenging the course record?"

"That's a 62, so it may be safe for another month. Anyway, greatness calls, I must obey."

"Keep in touch. You know Mary Louise; she never gets too far away from an ongoing investigation."

That evening Brad went through the files again. Round two. He kept thinking that he was missing something. A magic bullet where everything would fall into place. But it just was not there. Jake had been brutally killed and the hit and run vehicle had not been found. Okay, one more look in the morning.

The next morning over coffee, Brad went through it all once again. Nothing popped out. Maybe that was all there was. Time to move on. The value of the files depends on the quality of the responding officers and their ability to look past the obvious. Bullet in the chest? Yes, the man was shot. However, within that observation are many factors. How close? What angle? Where is the bullet? Other shots fired? The right officers on an initial response and a good crime scene team and you can have a trove of vital information.

The problem with this case was that the initial response was judged to be a hit and run right from the beginning, end of story. Guy got clipped by a speeding passing car. Other than the paint analysis not much more attention was paid to the victim's car. The crash scene was photographed but as it was night, the camera work was superficial and not very good. Brad was not sure they actually spent much time picking up debris from the scene other than to clear the road for the morning traffic. He could not blame them. It was late at night and the scene did not present anything more than a typical hit and run.

But the third time he looked through the files, the photos spoke to him! There were no skid marks from the car before it hit the vehicle and Jake. Also, and more telling, was the fact that the damage to Jake's car started at the driver's side door and went on through the front fender. It did not jump out when he read the police report but the photos were striking. Especially the ones from the rear of the victim's car. A picture may well be worth a thousand words! The hit and run vehicle must have swerved toward Jake's car or was purposely turned toward the car. Normally these kinds of "accidents" start at the rear of the victim's car, either directly crashing into the back of the car or on the corner of the car. Not here though. All the damage was in the front side part of the car. Brad reminded himself to not rush to judgement. Just another data point in the investigation. Too bad the victim's vehicle had been processed by the junkyard. If begged for more analysis.

The final file Brad reviewed was the autopsy report. Jake was mortally injured by the impact. Death had been instantaneous. Nobody could have survived that trauma. There were no marks or material embedded in his body that could give a clue to the make or model of the car that hit him All his personal effects had been listed in the police report and they did not provide any information either. So the upshot of Brad's review of the files was that the physical structure of the accident was odd. Maybe more than odd, but again Brad told himself, don't run ahead without the evidence.

Chapter 9

THE NEXT STEP IN THE investigation process was to list the players. In this case, not many at all. Linda Hagan and the children, her boyfriend, Jake's girlfriend and now the yardman at the salvage yard. Brad thought it best to start with the yardman. His call to Phil Raimondi at the police station had started their renewed interest in the case even though they could not put any manpower on it.

Salvage yards had always been of interest to Brad. Years back he had a car which was actually a Renault 9 built under license by the old American Motors Company back in the day. The car sold in the USA under the name Alliance. It was unreliable and that's being kind. The price was low but even so, too high for the quality of the car. It was a genuine dog, only exceeded by the Yugo which was a Fiat 127, built under license in the old Yugoslavia. Both bow-wows for sure. Brad had spent quite a bit of time in these yards pulling parts from busted up Alliances to keep his running. He was determined to get 125,000 miles out of his Alliance or die trying. Well, he made it - barely! Typically, when a car comes to the salvage yard, it is put out in the pasture. The wheels are taken off and all fluids drained from the car. Customers can then pick it over for parts. When they stop getting attention from the pickers, the engine is pulled out, the inside is stripped and the car is crushed in the "smasher". Just like in the old James Bond movie. After that, it's sold off by the pound as scrap.

When Brad arrived at the yard, He asked for Harry Shields, the guy who had made the call to Detective Raimondi. He was directed to "ChevyLand" in the north part of the field. Harry was a crusty guy who looked like he slept in his coveralls. Certainly did not take them off to wash very often.

"Harry Shields?"

"Yeah, who's asking?"

"My name is Brad Petronella; I work as an investigator for the DA's office. Can I ask you a few questions about the call you made to Detective Raimondi regarding the sugar in the gas tank of a 2012 Nissan Altima?"

"Sure, never thought I would hear anymore from you guys. What do you want to know?"

"Well I'd like to dig into the gasoline and sugar issue a bit and also ask if there was anything else that caught your attention."

Harry said "Well once the gas and sugar mix hits the fuel injectors, it really messes up an engine and depending on the mixture can cause overheating as the engine tries to keep running. It was strange to see a wrecked car with a load of sugar in it. Never seen that before. I told the boss and he said to call the cops."

"I am more interested in the timing of the matter. How long would the engine run after it has sugar in the tank?"

Harry said "Well like I told Mr. Prono at the DA's office already, if it had been in there a long time and there was a lot of it, you probably could not get the car started. If it had not been there for too long, you should be able to run the gas out of the fuel line and then maybe some from the tank before it kills the engine"

"Okay." Brad said "How many miles do you think it would run?"

Harry thought about this for a minute or so and then said, "As I said before to Detective Raimondi and the DA guy I would guess maybe between five and ten miles but after that, I think the engine would stop. Once it stops it's pretty much over. You couldn't get it started again."

Brad asked "Was there anything else you noticed about the car as you prepared it for the smasher?"

"Not really. It was pretty badly damaged on the left front side but the rest of the car was OK and the inside was pretty good too."

Brad answered. "Yeah, I saw the pictures from the police report. You know, I've spent a lot of time here some years back chasing down parts for my old Alliance."

"Alliance!" Harry said, "why would you buy that piece of crap?"

"Simple, money. We had three young kids, a mortgage, not making much. Want the rest of the story?"

"Nope, message received." Harry said, then he added, "You know that's the other thing I found odd."

"What do you mean?" asked Brad.

"That's the point," Harry said. "Money, the car was a good candidate for picking. The inside was clean and plenty of outside body left. Also, good tires, and the engine was OK. Transmission, engine mounts, battery was toast but there was still a lot of good stuff under the hood. We offered to put the car in the field for the pickers but she just wanted it crushed and gotten rid of. Which makes no sense because the boss has a nice program here. When we take in a car, we check it, and log its location in the field. Anytime a part is sold off the vehicle, the owner gets a small percentage. So, the boss pays for the scrap value of the car and also offers the owner a piece of the picking activity. The Altima is a popular car and would get good traffic."

"How much?" Brad asked.

"Maybe $75 and if the engine/transmission or seats and dash are sold it can go up to $250-$300. Ms. Hagan wasn't interested. All she wanted was to make it go away. Didn't care about anything else. So we stripped out what we could and scrapped the rest in the smasher. Funny, I thought the car might be a mule in drug distribution because she was so hot to get rid of it but when we stripped it out, it was clean and didn't show any hiding places. Trust me, we've seen them all over the years. We offered her $25 and that was the deal."

"Thanks," Brad said, "you've been very helpful. Would you be willing to meet with the DA at some point if she wants to get this all down in a deposition?"

"What's a deposition?"

"It is a sworn statement that can be presented to a grand jury or used in a court proceeding."

"Can do."

Brad thanked Harry for his time and the information. So, he thought, we have a compromised fuel system and an eager interest in a quick salvage operation.

Chapter 10

THE NEXT STOP IN THE tour would be to talk with Spud and Mary Lou about what he found out to date and get some background information on the ex-wife and her boyfriend. So, he put in a call to Spud.

"Spud, what's your calendar look like? I want to meet you and the DA to update you on my progress so far and get background information on Linda Hagan and Bodie Varilly.

"What, you are not out on the golf course?"

Brad replied "No, season is pretty much over and I'm working for you to earn the large salary you're paying me."

"OK come on over Monday at 11:00. We'll be finished with a staff meeting and I can have some lunch bought in. Can it hold till then?"

"Sure, I need some time to tidy up my notes and thoughts. How are you doing? You sound a bit down. Are you feeling OK?"

"I'm OK but I'm worried about my son Jaime. He keeps running away from his mother's house over to me and seems so angry all the time. He always spends time with me on the weekends but now everything is a problem for him. He's angry with both of us and his school grades are headed south. Also, his friends are starting to worry me. They're not the ones he's grown up with and I don't like their attitude. We've tried to talk with him but he doesn't want to open up at all"

Brad said, "sorry to hear that. Jaime always struck me as a good kid and he's smart. He can pretty much do whatever he wants, he has the horsepower."

"That may be," Spud said "but he sure isn't firing on all cylinders these days. Tell you what. One weekend a month the three of us get together for dinner, keep the family thing going. This weekend is our time for the family dinner, can you come over and join us? I know Erin would love to see you, it's been some time since we all were together and I would like to get your thoughts on Jaime."

"That would be fun, let's do it. LuLu is out of town at a writers' conference over the weekend, so it's a good fit."

"Thanks," said Spud. "I really need a third party to take a look at this. Maybe talk some sense into Jaime."

"Wish it were that simple," Brad said "Let's just enjoy our time together and see what plays out. I don't want to put Jaime on stage. If he thinks we've got an agenda, he will clam up and we'll never know what's happening. Just remember, I have grown children and grandchildren so I am a certified expert!"

"Yes 'oh wise one', your guidance is my path!"

Chapter 11

THE RELATIONSHIP BETWEEN Spud and Erin was curious. They were not actually divorced or even formally separated. They still shared the same bank accounts for household expenses and each was the other's beneficiary on the insurances. Brad always thought they were too young, around twenty, when they married. They were both still kids in college. During the course of their 15-year marriage, they had both grown up and clearly were not the same people anymore.

They had been living apart for a little over a year and Spud thought they were trying to find themselves. Maybe they had to meet again and fall in love? There was no outward friction between them now that they were living apart. They shared the parenting responsibilities without reservation and were committed to Jaime. He was loved by both of them and was not used as a weapon or crutch between them. Since living apart, neither one had found a significant other and Spud felt neither of them was looking for anyone either.

They met that Saturday at Erin's house which was the one they had lived in before the separation. It was a nice ranch on a good size lot with oaks and maples in the front and backyard. It was all on one floor. Brad was getting to like the idea of everything on one floor as he grew older. He thought, *I have one more move in me and it better be to a place all on one floor.* Just like LuLu, Erin's style was eclectic. Nothing matched but everything fit. It was a warm comfortable place. Spud was on the back deck firing up the grille. Steak tonight thought Brad. Good, maybe NY strips.

Erin came out on the deck. "What can I get you? We have red, white, and even some Ballantine's."

"Oh you remembered," said Brad. "Ice, half soda, half scotch in a large old-fashioned glass."

"Don't worry, I haven't forgotten."

While Brad and Spud were solving the problems of the world on the back deck, Jaime came out and joined them.

Jaime was in his last year of middle school and seemed to grow taller by the minute. Spud was close to 6 foot 4 inches and Jaime seemed well on his way to capture the title. He was all arms and legs and nothing seemed to fit yet, but you could see a strapping kid in the making.

"Jaime, you look great, how is your basketball game coming along?"

"I'm not playing much these days, sort of busy with my friends," he replied, looking down.

"Too bad," said Brad. "You have a great sense of the court and good hand eye coordination, hate to see it go to waste. Maybe play some summer league?"

"Maybe," Jaime said.

"Think about it." Brad said. "Hit 9th grade with a fade away jump shot and you own the place!"

"You think so?"

Brad replied "Sure, with your height you can play under the rim and with the jump shot you could also play out near the arc. Big guy with soft hands playing inside and outside is a tough combination."

"H'mm, maybe," said Jaime.

"Don't sit on it," Brad said, "You'll need summer league experience to see what the other kids in the area have as you'll be up against them in high school."

Dinner was a treat. NY strips, creamed spinach, baked potato and great conversation. They didn't press Jaime on what was going on in his life. They treated him as an equal in the conversations and he enjoyed himself. Well Spud thought, this could be a good baseline for further conversations with the boy should the opportunity arise. Brad left around 10PM. It was not a long drive to his place.

Surprisingly, as he was walking in the door, the phone rang and it was Spud.

"Sorry to call like this but just wanted to thank you and see what your thoughts were about Jaime."

Well, the kid definitely needs to develop a fade away jump shot," said Brad.

"Come on man, you know where I want to go," joked Spud.

"Sure, I do. Let me think about this for a bit. I think I have an idea but it involves all of you. This is a family problem and needs a family solution."

"Okay," Spud said," happy you're a player in this. Let us know. See you on Monday."

Chapter 12

BRAD, SPUD AND MARY Louise sat around the conference table in her office. Lunch was sandwiches, chips, coleslaw and potato salad. Nice spread, a lot more than he was used to eating at lunch. So, make sure dinner is light.

"OK," Mary Louise said, "what have you found out so far?"

"Well," Brad replied, "a lot of relatively small points but they all seem to add up to something more than just a hit and run. The closer I get to this the more I find that a hit and run doesn't ring true. We may not have the smoking gun yet but certainly lots of kindling to light a fire."

"Fill us in please," said Spud.

"OK, let me list what I have so far." said Brad. "First of all, the accident scene photos don't show any skid marks ahead of the hit. Maybe the driver didn't see Jake but there is usually some indication of a driver trying to stop or swerve out of the way. Also, the damage to the car was on the driver side door and front fender area, nothing on the back of the car or along the rear side. Just the front door and front left fender. Sure he could have drifted over and hit Jake, but it seems more of a glancing blow, not really consistent with hit and runs we usually see. Second, the car is actually registered to Linda Hagan. Maybe nothing there, but I would expect the vehicle to be in Jake's name. That's how it's shown in the divorce decree. But if it was hers, why was he driving the car? The fact that the car was registered in her name gave her control over its disposition at the salvage yard and her actions on that are strange."

"How so?" asked Spud.

"Well in talking to Harry Shields at Downs Salvage, it seems that after the yard got the wreck from the Sheriff, he called Linda Hagan and

"

told her they had the car. He told her that they would put the car in the field and let parts pickers have access to it before they put it in the smasher. He explained to her that the owner had a scheme that paid the vehicle owner a small percentage for any parts recovered from the car. She might make around $100-200 on it and then a salvage price would be paid. Also, if major parts were recovered from the car, she could make more money, maybe $250-$300. As the car was an Altima and popular, Harry felt that it would get a lot of traffic from pickers. The salvage yard also sent her a letter outlining the offer. However, she wanted nothing to do with any of this. She said just put the car in the smasher and get it done quickly. So, they cut a deal for $25 and that was the end of it. Third, you already know about the sugar in the gas tank. It would give it 5-10 miles before the engine conked out. If you wanted it to stop on the Colesville Road, which is deserted at night, you could have fixed it that way.

"How could anyone be sure he was going home from his girlfriend's house and he'd be on that road?" Spud asked.

"Good question," said Brad. "I need to dig into this."

Brad continued, "So as you can see, more questions keep surfacing. I am not comfortable that we are dealing with a simple hit and run at this point. Maybe it will all fall into place but there are a lot of parts that just don't fit."

"I agree," said Mary Louise, "what are the next steps?"

"Well," Brad said, "I need to interview Linda Hagan and Bodie Varilly. Also, Carol Barnett who was Jake's girlfriend. However, before I do this can you get me some background information on them. Bodie is of particular interest; we don't know anything about him other than his name."

"I'll put it together and get back to you," said Spud.

"Thanks, the sooner the better."

"Okay," said Mary Louise, "I agree with you about what you have found so far. Let's keep it rolling. I have to split now. Court in 30 minutes and I have a new ADA going in front of Judge Carmichael."

"A real Judge Judy," said Spud. "Trial by fire."

Chapter 13

WITH THE MEETING CONCLUDED, Brad headed home. LuLu would be getting back from the writers' conference in New York City and he was eager to see how things had gone. She had been going to meet a potential agent who seemed like a good fit. A good agent made all the difference in dealing with book publishers. Chasing publishers was tedious and in many cases a waste of time. They usually did not have the staff to properly review material and spent a lot of time chasing the latest book fad. Now they all seemed preoccupied with fantasy novels and superheroes. He thought it was a somewhat sad commentary on society today. Also, Tasha would be demanding a run in the woods chasing squirrels and rabbits. She never caught any but the chase was the real show.

LuLu was there when he got home.

"So did you sign with a killer agent and gain access to all the major publishing houses?" asked Brad.

"Not quite," said LuLu "but the one I met specializes in my genre' and has been in the business a long time. Knows her way around. Small to middle size operation with a good stable of writers. If I can get on with her, I should be able to get some good exposure and who knows, a book contract too. I liked her. She was very practical about what could happen and also the timeline in this business. Nothing happens tomorrow, not even the day after that. But once the ball gets rolling, it can be quite rewarding. And as I said, I like the writers she represents. They are all successful. She also represents script writers for TV and movies but I've never done anything like that, so for now, I will stay with the novels."

"But if they take a book to a movie script, don't they have people who do that?" asked Brad.

"Yes, there are writers who do that but it is way out in the future for me and so far she hasn't even offered to represent me for my books!"

"Don't worry," said Brad "I'll call her up and tell her she is missing the opportunity of a lifetime if she doesn't take you on!"

"Great, thanks," said LuLu. That should seal the deal!".

In the warmth of a late Fall afternoon, they changed into well-worn clothes and headed off to familiar trails with Tasha who, as always, lived in hope of a big score with the squirrels. From all the noise the squirrels made, Brad was sure they were laughing at her. Didn't matter to Tasha, she was on the hunt, so squirrels beware! Most of the leaves had turned color and the colors were getting dull which meant that shortly they would be falling. The poplar trees had already dropped most of their leaves. They were always late in the spring and early out in the fall. It was a beautiful afternoon. Sun, the smell of the leaves on the ground, LuLu by his side, so far from the hit and run with all the loose ends. That was for another day. Right now the trick was to stay in the moment. After the walk, a quiet dinner, movie on Netflix and catching up on some reading in bed.

It took a few days for the personnel files on Linda, Bodie and Carol to come in. However, by mid-week, Brad had what he needed. The files on the two women were not compelling. They were both from the area and other than a few traffic violations, nothing popped out on an initial read. Bodie was different. He was from another county further west in the state. His family had farmed over there from the mid-1800's, having come from Connecticut. Both the state of New York and Connecticut were victims of the ice age, with lots of rocks making the land difficult to work. But Brad guessed New York was better or at least the Varillys had thought so.

Bodie had been in and out of trouble since he was a juvenile. Truancy, fighting, and as he grew older, more serious problems. He had three assault charges in his jacket. One was dropped and the other two were listed as aggravated assault. One, a bar fight and the other involved road rage. He had been in and out of county jail over the years. His credit rating was poor and he was carrying a lot of credit card debt. Also, he had a general discharge from the Army. Not a dishonorable discharge, but still not good. Clearly, the Army was fed up with him for whatever reason and wanted him out of the service. Bodie made his money by doing small contracting jobs. Anything from handyman work to foundations and small additions. There was no evidence of problems with his work. Maybe he was clever with his hands and not so much with his head. Brad would speak to Bodie last. He still needed to look into the family further. He would go over to Tompkins county, look around and speak with the Sheriff but he decided to speak with Jake's girlfriend first. Based on what he saw in the files, she seemed to be the cleanest in terms of history.

Chapter 14

BRAD CALLED CAROL BURNETT, introduced himself and said he wanted to talk about the hit and run that killed her fiancé. She was still trying to come to terms with what happened to Jake and was happy to provide whatever help she could. She lived in a small raised ranch in a quiet neighborhood off Court St. The house and the grounds were well maintained.

"How long have you lived here?" asked Brad.

"Well," replied Carol, "let me see. Must be all of twelve years now. I moved here right after I took a job at the electric company. I got my accounting degree from Binghamton University and started soon after. I'd interned with them for two summers so we sort of knew each other. It's been a good fit and I enjoy the work."

"Any relationships before Jake?" Brad asked. He knew she was not married from the files but wanted to see how she would react to the question.

"Not really," Carol said, "I was in a long-term relationship with a guy but he never wanted to take it any further. So, I reached the point where I needed to get on with my life. I wasn't necessarily looking to get married but I didn't want to spend the rest of my life with a guy who only wanted to be a good friend. I've had a good social life since then but nothing clicked. Then I met Jake at a friend's house. He was recently divorced with two children as I'm sure you know. At first I didn't want to get involved with a divorced man with two children. It seemed like a recipe for disaster. He was just as careful as me as it turned out. He was afraid of falling into another bad relationship. He has been married for twelve years and the last five were grim. In the end, he had to get out. I don't know his wife so what I am telling you has been filtered through Jake, you understand?"

"Understood," replied Brad.

"Well," Carol continued. " It seems as if Linda was extremely manipulative and had been having affairs throughout their marriage. She could spend money like a drunken sailor and Jake was always trying to clear debt."

Brad asked "Was Bodie part of any of these affairs?"

"Yes and in fact they've had a relationship for the better part of four years," Carol replied. "Jake told me that Bodie first came on the scene when they had some trees removed from the backyard of their house on Colesville Road. I don't know specific dates for their affairs but I believe it was an on and off again relationship."

"Anything else?" asked Brad

"The divorce was not finalized on good terms," said Carol. "Jake said that it was a difficult process even though he wasn't contesting the distribution of the assets or any support responsibilities. However, once Linda found out about our relationship, things became almost impossible. Linda made unrealistic demands to the point where Jake pulled back and told his attorney to settle it based on his best judgement and what the court would approve. He just wanted to get away from her and get on with his life. It was an emotional roller coaster for him. He would come over to the house sometimes and just sit without speaking. He was drained."

"Tell me about the last night he was here," prompted Brad.

"Well," said Carol, "we always had dinner here on Friday night. It seemed like a nice way to end the week and plan for the weekend. The kids were usually with us on weekends and we wanted to make sure we planned their activities. Linda didn't mind Jake having the kids on the weekend. I think she was fed up with them by the time Friday came around. She was not a warm person."

"Were they with you on that night?" asked Brad.

"No, it was Gary's birthday and Linda insisted that they spend the evening with her. Jake had agreed to pick them up on Saturday morning in time for Gary's soccer game."

"Where was Jake's car parked that night?"

"On the street at the end of my lot. I was having the driveway sealed and the guys needed it clear and they also needed room for their truck and equipment."

Brad went over to the front door and looked out at where Jake had parked his car. The corner of the lot was in a semi wooded area and there weren't any houses around it.

Brad asked," Do you remember which direction the car was facing? When you looked at it did you see the front or rear of the car?"

"Oh it was the front. He always came down the street in that direction and just pulled over to the side along my property line. Why? Is that important?"

"I don't know at this stage," replied Brad, "just trying to get a clear picture."

But privately he thought it would have been pretty easy for someone to get next to the car and tamper with the fuel without being seen. The tank was filled from the driver's side.

Brad thanked Carol for her time and cooperation and told her that she might be asked to meet with the DA and provide a formal statement.

As he was leaving Carol asked, "it seems clear that you're not happy with the findings in this accident. Are you looking at more than a hit and run?"

Brad told her that at this point they were tying up loose ends and he'd see where the evidence took him. Carol didn't press the question but was ready to believe there were other factors in play.

Chapter 15

THE NEXT DAY BRAD DROVE past Linda's house later in the afternoon. It was a simple place on a spacious lot as was the custom in the town. Land was not an issue. Kids toys were in the front and side yard and he could see a young boy shooting baskets in the driveway. He had a nice touch with the ball and dribbled with either hand without looking at the ball. He was maybe two or three years younger than Jaime. Both would go to the same high school – Binghamton. He wondered if he could put the two of them together. They didn't live too far away from each other. Well, another issue for another time thought Brad. He parked on the street so as to not disturb Gary in the driveway. Linda must have seen him coming as she answered the door right after he rang the bell.

"Good afternoon," he said. "My name is Brad Petronella and I work for the District Attorney. I would like to ask you some questions about the recent death of your ex-husband Jake."

Linda replied "I ain't got nothing to say and certainly don't plan on speaking with you or anyone from the DA's office. So why don't you just get off my property or I'll call the police."

"Ms. Hagan," Brad said, "here is how this plays out. You can talk with me now or I can get a subpoena issued to compel you to meet with the District Attorney. That will take place at her convenience in her office. I strongly suggest that if you choose that course of action, you retain an attorney. If we talk now, it's informal. Your call on how we move forward. Personally, I don't care what you decide but we will meet and you will answer our questions."

Faced with the prospect of a more formal meeting with the District Attorney, Linda replied, "Okay, let's talk now and get this over. I don't really know anything about this other than what I read in the papers and heard on TV. So, ask your questions."

"Thank you. Can I come inside?"

As they were sitting down in the kitchen, the two children Gary and Darlene came in and asked if they could watch TV before dinner. Linda told them it was OK but to keep the noise down. The kids went into the family room and started watching something from YouTube.

"I noticed that the car Jake was driving the night of the accident was a Nissan Altima," began Brad, "but from reading the divorce decree, it states that the car was to be yours. Do I understand that correctly?"

Linda said, "Well yes but we, that is Jake and me, decided to switch cars as I needed the Equinox for the kids. I am always hauling stuff around to their sports and camps. I needed more space. We were going to get the registrations changed at some point."

"I see," said Brad. "Now about a month after the accident Downs Salvage Yard called to tell you they had the vehicle and asked about the disposal of the car?"

"Something like that," said Linda. "I don't keep a calendar on this stuff. Yeah they did call and tell me they had the car and what did I want to do with it. So what, who cares at this point. It was all banged up."

"Did Downs discuss with you any options you might have regarding the disposition of the vehicle?"

"No," said Linda. "Just they had it and were going to send it to the smasher."

"That's not what they told me," said Brad. "They said they offered to put the car in the field for pickers and pay you a percentage of the sale of parts off the car. At some point it would be picked over and then would go to the smasher. Given that the Altima is a popular car, they felt there were a few dollars to be made in leaving it in the field for a bit. In fact, they sent you a letter about all of this."

"So what?" said Linda "who cares about that stupid old wrecked car? I could do whatever I wanted with it."

"Sure you could," said Brad, "but why not make a buck or two from it? What was the rush Linda? It wasn't not going anywhere."

"Look Mr. Petro-fella," said Linda, "I could do whatever I wanted with it and I don't have to answer to you. So back off and go chase some bank robbers."

"What are you hiding Linda?" asked Brad.

By this time Linda was becoming agitated and her voice had risen and brought the children into the kitchen. Brad couldn't continue the interview with her in this state and didn't want to worry the children. So he thanked her for her time and prepared to leave. As he was picking up his papers, he said, "Can I ask you one more question before I leave?"

"Can I stop you?" Linda said "Go ahead."

"Where were you and Bodie on the night that Jake was hit?"

"We were both here and Bodie spent the night."

"No Mom," said Gary. "It was my birthday and we went out for pizza and then to a movie, remember? Bodie wasn't here."

"Yes he was," said Linda.

"No Mommy," said Darlene "Gary and I remember, it was his birthday and you had promised us to go out, just the three of us."

"Okay, so what," said Linda, "who cares anyway. Here, there, no big deal. Time for you to go Mr. Petro-fella, I got dinner to make."

Brad thanked her for her time and left the house. So, he thought, interesting. She was in a hurry to get rid of the car and clearly lied about Bodie being with them the night Jake was killed. As always in these investigations, it was little steps, little steps that lead you to a bigger result. Brad felt he had taken it about as far as he could with Linda at this point. Time to move on to Bodie. After Bodie, the Tompkins County Sheriff.

Chapter 16

FINDING BODIE PROVED a bit of a problem. He had an address for Bodie, but he never seemed to be at home. Brad finally found him at a local watering hole on upper State Street. For want of a better term, it was his local. Brad found him at the bar with a couple of like-minded gentlemen. Brad introduced himself and asked if he could ask him some questions about the death of Jake Hagan.

Bodie said, "Well lookee here a hot shot dick wanting to talk with me. What did I do, rob a bank, steal an old lady's purse, forget to pay a parking ticket?"

Brad responded, "Okay Bodie, I see you're a big-time asshole, we can talk here or downtown with the DA. If you go that way, I'll tell you the same thing I told Linda. If you want to meet downtown with the DA, get a lawyer. So what do you want to do shithead? Impress the bar flies here and meet up later with the DA?"

The wind taken out of his sails Bodie responded, "OK let's sit over there in the booth."

To make sure Bodie understood the drill, Brad explained to him that they were trying to close out the hit and run on Jake Hagan. Bodie seemed to be agreeable with the line of questions and apparently did not see any threat.

"So," Brad said, "Tell me about you and Linda Hagan".

"Not much to say," Bodie replied, "we got together after her divorce from Jake. Pretty much only seeing each other now."

"Did you know here before?" asked Brad.

"Not really," said Bodie, "I did some work for them over the years."

"Just work?" asked Brad.

"What are you getting at?" Bodie asked. "What happened between us is our business and I ain't going into any detail for you. None of your goddamn business. Next question."

"DMV records show you have a nice new ride, big Chevy Tahoe," said Brad.

"Sure do my man," said Bodie. My ride was stolen a while back."

"What kind of car? Was it ever recovered?"

"Toyota Camry and never found," said Bodie. "but you already know that, I bet."

"Camry?" Brad said, "Sort of a sissy car for a big stud like you don't you think?"

"Took it off a guy who owed me for some contracting work," Bodie said. "He was broke and couldn't pay cash so I took the next best thing."

"Bet the girls loved you in the Camry", said Brad.

"Screw you."

"By the way," Brad said, "what color was the Toyota?"

"How the hell do I know?" Bodie said, "some kind of white, who cares?"

"I do," said Brad "I really do."

At this point Bodie was getting nervous with the line of questioning and wanted out.

"That's it for now big guy," he told Brad. "I'm done answering your dumb ass questions. I've got better things to do".

"One last question." said Brad, "Where were you on the night of October 10th?"

"How the hell do I know? I ain't got no social secretary," said Bodie.

"The night Jake Hagan was killed," said Brad. "Surely you can remember that."

"Oh yeah," said Bodie, "spent it at Linda's."

"Really," Brad said, "not what the kids say. It was Gary's birthday and they were all out for a family evening, pizza and a movie."

"Oh yeah," said Bodie "came over after and spent the night."

"Not what the kids say." Brad replied. "Guess they're lying, can't trust the little dudes these days."

"Screw you, all you are trying to do is trap me. I ain't talking to you no more. Fuck off!" said Bodie.

"Thanks for your time," said Brad and he left the bar with Bodie trying to figure out what he knew. Bodie needed to get back to Linda and make sure she held her ground and didn't change her story.

Chapter 17

WHEN BODIE GOT TO LINDA'S house, he found her in the kitchen. The kids were over with her sister and would be back after dinner.

"What did you tell that investigator dick from the DA?" demanded Bodie.

"Nothing," said Linda. "He wanted to know about the car Jake was driving and why it was still in my name. I told him we swapped out cars as I needed the Equinox for space for the kid's junk. He also asked about why I got it scrapped so quickly when I could have left it in the field for the pickers".

"What about me staying the night here when Jake was whacked?" asked Bodie

"Told him you were with me," said Linda

"Ain't what the kids said," Brad replied, "and I think he likes the kids story a lot better than yours."

"They're just kids," said Linda, "what do they know?"

"A lot," said Bodie "and I don't like it."

Linda could see this falling apart and was getting worried. She knew the kids had the date locked down as it was Gary's birthday and this left Bodie without an alibi if things really went south.

"Why did you have to kill him Bodie?" she said. "The plan was to beat him up. Why did you do it?"

"I saw an opportunity and took it," said Bodie. "Dumb ass was standing almost in the middle of the road. I meant to knock him off to the side with the car but when I accelerated, he ran toward the front of his car and I lost it a bit when I swerved toward him. He bounced off the front door of his car. Wrong place to be I guess."

"This investigator guy is no fool Bodie, we really need to be careful with what we say to him," replied Linda.

"Well I ain't talking to him again," said Bodie, "they're gonna have to arrest me or something. And you do the same, no more talking!"

Bodie had always been a loose cannon. He ran by his emotions and never thought things through. On top of it, he had a bad temper and it had been the source of many of his problems over the years. Linda felt she could keep the relationship under control and when she divorced Jake, he was there to step in. But this turn of events was not good, to say the least. Bodie had killed someone. She did not really care about Jake and wanted revenge for his leaving her. And it was not even for another woman, he just wanted out of their marriage. *'My fault?'* No way she thought. *'He screwed me over and got what he deserved. Served him right.'* But Bodie was too unstable and she was worried where this was all going.

Chapter 18

TOMPKINS COUNTY WAS not the next county over from Broome county, Brad had to go through Tioga county first and then north. About a 45-minute drive from his house. He always enjoyed the country around central NY. Rolling hills, some small farms left, even a few dairy farms remained. But things had changed and it was a painful adjustment for folks. When a region loses an industry, the industry does not come back. Manufacturing, agriculture had one thing in common - they gravitated to cheaper labor markets and/or more economical production. For a region to make a comeback, it has to reinvent itself. Not an easy thing to do and it takes time.

When he arrived at Sheriff Hodges office in Tompkins County he was a welcome visitor.

"I remember you from your detective days on the force in Binghamton and also with the DA," said Sheriff Hodges. "I like your DA. Wish we had her here. We are still stuck with a good old boy who'll get reelected until he falls over or we enter the next ice age."

Brad asked, "Why is that? There must be some younger talent around here,"

"Well I guess there is," the Sheriff said, "but the job doesn't pay much and with the decline in population, we're a county of older folks that don't want a change. The DA is from an old family here and people are familiar with the name and face. But you didn't come here to talk about local politics, did you? Spud called and gave me a heads up so I have put together some information on the Varillys."

"Thanks," Brad said, "one of them keeps coming up in my investigation."

"Don't tell me," the Sheriff said, "Bodie."

"That's the guy," Brad said "but why him?"

"Well he's the worst of the lot," the Sheriff said. "Family has been here for generations on the same land. The first Varillys came over from Connecticut. Farmed the land for generations until farming just would not pay anymore. The last of them, Bodie and some of his cousins, are still around and are the bottom of the barrel. I've had them in my jail numerous times. Mostly for fighting, drinking, petty stuff, but some of them have a real mean streak. Bodie for sure. One of the reasons he doesn't live here anymore is that I told him the next time in jail would be a long stretch. I guess he got the message and moved on. Been gone about four years now. I see Bodie in and around town but he doesn't live here now. His cousin Will Varilly still lives on the land outside of town. Over the years they've sold off a lot of it but they still have around 150 acres off Stewart Road. Will survives doing odd jobs and small contracting work.

"Hmm," Brad thought, "same as Bodie."

The Sheriff said "The place is a dump. Double wide trailer needing repairs and junk scattered all over the place. Old farm equipment, junk cars and God knows what else. A well in front of the place for water and septic in the back for waste. Maybe it will all run together and take them all out. I don't know what they do out there but whatever it is can't be legal, they wouldn't know how to do it."

"Drugs?" said Brad.

"Maybe," said the Sheriff. "We thought they might be running a meth lab but couldn't find any evidence of it. I actually flew my nephew's drone over the land looking for a separate building or a heat source. We didn't find anything. We're very careful about chemical purchases in the county given all the meth in play but nothing tying it to the Varillys."

"Could they be a waypoint on a drug distribution network, or sell drugs?" asked Brad.

"My deputy asked the same question, Brad," said Sheriff Hodges, "we're looking in that direction. I think you should go out and talk to

Will and see what you can find out about Bodie. If you see anything interesting, let me know."

"I'll do that," said Brad. "I'll check back with you before I leave town."

It was the middle of the afternoon when Brad got to the farm, or what was left of it. As the Sheriff said, the double wide trailer had seen better days. The weather-beaten barns still stood on the lot about 40 yards from the double wide. There was junk scattered all over the place, cars, farm equipment and an assortment of tools, children's yard swings, wading pools and bikes. Seems as if they were just dropped and people walked away.

Nobody was around. Brad didn't know if there were still children around, or maybe a Mrs. Varilly living there. He drove around the buildings looking for Will but no joy. As he was turning around he noticed a white Toyota in one of the barns. Clearly banged up. It was not covered in dust and dirt so it looked like it hadn't been there for very long. He didn't go into the barn but looked from the outside. The front right portion was clearly heavily damaged but he couldn't see all of it as it was against the wall. The left side was visible but that wasn't the side that would have hit Jake. Better do this by the book Brad thought, get a search warrant. As Brad was walking back to his car to leave, someone drove up. Will Varilly.

He was not happy to see anyone on his property. He got out of his car saying, "Who the hell are you and what do you want? This is private property and you have no right to be here. Why were you in the barn?"

"I wasn't in the barn and if you're Varilly, I'm actually looking for you," said Brad. "I'm doing some work for the DA in Broome County and would like to ask you some questions."

"I'm Varilly. What questions?" asked Will, "I ain't done nothing."

"Didn't say you had." said Brad, "Not you, Bodie."

"What's that asshole done now?" said Will.

"I don't know," said Brad, "just trying to fill in some holes in an ongoing case".

"Maybe I don't want to talk to you," said Will.

"I don't care." said Brad, "Talk to me or talk to the Sheriff, whatever works for you. And as I told your cousin Bodie, if you want to talk with the Sheriff, lawyer up my man"

"So, what do you want to know?" said Will "I don't see a lot of Bodie these days."

"Has he been around lately?"

"Yeah," said Will, "a few weeks back."

"What did he want?" asked Brad

"Nothing special, just was in the area and stopped by."

"How much property do you have here?"

"A little less than 150 acres. We have a perimeter road around the land from the farming days and a couple of ponds and old quarry on the western part," said Will grudgingly. "We don't farm the land anymore."

"How do you get by?"

"Odd jobs, small contracting, pouring foundations, this and that,"

"You do anything with Bodie?"

"Not really, he does his thing and I do mine."

"Who owns the property?"

"Three of us," said Will. "Me, Bodie and my sister Ruth who lives downstate near the city, we don't see her no more".

Good for her thought Brad, best stay away from these two. There was not much more to ask Will. The Toyota in the barn was the immediate interest and he needed a search warrant to get to the car. He thanked Will for his time and left the property. While driving away from Will he called Sheriff Hodges.

"Sheriff, I need a search warrant for the Varilly property. I think I may have found the car involved in the Jake Hagan hit and run. I need a crime scene team to look at it and run the VIN. I think Bodie hid it here after the accident, if we can still call it that."

"Okay Brad," the Sheriff said, "let me call Judge Thomas and get a warrant issued. What are you going to do?"

"I'll head over to your office. I'll fill you in on the details so you can write a tight search warrant request. I don't want this to slip away on us. Can you also call Spud at the DA's office in Binghamton and let him know where I am and what our next steps are?"

On the way out, Brad decided to drive along the perimeter road to get a feel for the place. Since no farming had been done there for a number of years the fields were all overgrown. There were a couple of ponds and even an old gravel quarry, long filled in with water. Probably a great swimming hole. Cold water and deep he thought. Turning a corner on the far west portion of the property, he noticed there was a landing strip there. Not paved, no lights but clearly the ground had been levelled, compacted and any drainage issues sorted out. Thinking back to his flying days, Brad guessed it was around 3500 feet. Hard to see but there it was. The approach on both ends of the runway was over a wooded area. This was not an abandoned runway. It was in good repair and showed evidence of being used. He could see tire tracks, probably from a plane's main landing gear. At one end of the field in the woods was an old tractor with a grader attached to it. He guessed it was used to keep the runway in reasonable shape.

What are you bad boys doing? thought Brad, clearly not running a Delta Airlines operation.

Chapter 19

THE PERIMETER ROAD took him back by Will's double wide on the way out. As he came up to the trailer, he saw the exit onto the county road blocked by Will's truck. Will was standing next to it with a shotgun. He came over to the driver's side of Brad's car.

"Out of the car, Mr. Investigator and keep your hands where I can see them," he said.

Right after Brad left, Will called his cousin to let him know that Brad had been there and was asking a lot of questions. When Will mentioned he first saw him standing by the barn looking at the Toyota, Bodie knew it was only a question of time before they tied the car and the hit and run to him. Too much at stake here, Brad had to be dealt with immediately. If a lab got hold of the Toyota, he was toast. When Will told him Brad had turned south and was driving the perimeter road Bodie knew he would have to pass the house again on the way out.

"Block the road and get him in the barn. Tie him up," said Bodie. "I'll be there in forty-five minutes. We'll take care of him after dark. Dump him in the quarry."

"I ain't getting involved in no killings, Bodie. You whacked Jake and now you want to do the same to this investigator guy. I ain't playing," said Will.

"The hell you ain't involved," said Bodie. "We been running drugs off this place for five years and now this investigator shows up wondering about that asshole Jake? Fuck this. The DA guy is going to disappear, the fucking Toyota is going away and we stay in business. You dumb shit, I told you to get rid of the car and what did you do - you parked it in the barn. That car should have been at the bottom of the quarry weeks ago you dumb bastard. So, now we are going to clean this all up once and for all!"

Now, as he got out of the car Brad said, "Will, do you really want to do this? Bodie is going down. He probably killed Jake Hagan and now you want to be involved in a murder? Don't be stupid! He'll take you down with him. You're looking at serious jail in the Big House, Attica. Use your head Will, this will not end well for you."

"Shut up!" said Will, "there is more to this than you understand. Bodies right, we gotta clean this up."

Brad said, "I am pretty sure you guys are running drugs out of here. For yourselves and maybe some distribution network. I saw the airstrip. So you offer a drive and fly service as the local distributor. I bet you're real popular with the boys down south."

"Shut your mouth, I said," Will growled. "I don't care what you know or think. You're going away, end of story."

Of all things, Will had a pair of handcuffs. Got them on the Internet one time. He had Brad lay on his stomach while will pointed the gun at the back of his head.

"Put your hands on your back. Try anything funny and I'll blow your head off!"

He put the cuffs on Brad, took him to the barn and finished by tying him to a support pole. He took his cell phone and smashed it.

"You ain't going nowhere," he said to the prisoner.

Brad said nothing. He just slipped down to the ground, his back against the pole, wondering how the hell he was going to get out of this one.

Chapter 20

SHERIFF HODGES HAD the boilerplate of the search warrant drafted. Location, names of individuals, relationship to a crime, search parameters, etc. He needed Brad to put the final touches on it so they could get it to the Judge. He had been called and alerted that a search warrant was coming for his review and signature. But where was Brad? He should have been here over an hour ago. The Sheriff called Spud at the DA's office.

"Has Brad checked in with you Spud?" asked the Sheriff.

"No," said Spud "Last call I got was from you. What's going on? Is he OK? Has there been an accident?"

"I don't know any more than he was supposed to be here over an hour ago to help finish off the wording on a search warrant for the Varilly farm. I have a team ready to go. I checked with the State Police and they don't know of any accidents on the roads, so I can only assume he's still at the farm. Look, you guys see if you can find Bodie and if you do keep eyes on him. I'll take my SWAT team and head out to the farm."

Spud immediately called Lt. Raimondi at the Binghamton police and updated him. The detective put out an APB on Bodie, who he had already left for the farm.

When Bodie arrived, his cousin took him to the barn to check on Brad. As Will said earlier, he wasn't going anywhere. Brad did not try to speak with Bodie. He was too unstable. The last thing he wanted was him doing something rash on the spur of the moment. He needed to buy some time. That is all he had at this point. His eyes closed, he sent silent messages to Sheriff Hodges. Surely the man had missed him by now?

"What are we going to do?" asked Will.

"We'll keep him here until it's dark and then put him in the trunk of the Toyota," said Bodie. "Then we'll drop'em both in the quarry. Which is where you were supposed to put the Toyota a month ago, asshole. It's over a hundred feet deep, no one will ever find him or the car."

Back in town, the Sheriff got the SWAT team together and briefed them on the operation. "Okay, guys," he said, "this is now a tactical operation and not a search. Everyone put on your vests and helmets, make sure you have all your gear. We are going out to the Varilly farm and I have no idea what to expect. But we don't want to come up short. There could be a lot of guns out there. Once the operation starts, Sgt. Woods will be the on-site tactical commander and he will direct the operation. He'll run the show. Understood?"

Sergeant Woods stood up. "When we get there, there is no easy or discreet way to get on to the property so use the vehicles to split the barn and double wide. Secure the barn and then establish a perimeter around the double wide. I'm betting they're in one or the other. Hopefully, our investigator also. When you come onto the property, drive in fast and move quickly. I don't want to give them a chance to move."

"Sirens?" asked one of the techs.

"No," said Sgt. Woods, "I don't want them to hear us coming. There is no way to get on the property without them seeing us. But if we're quick, we take their reaction time away. We can use flash-bangs if we need to storm the trailer. Okay? Everyone on board?"

They went to the farm in three vehicles. Total of ten personnel with two dogs and equipment. When they got to the property, they quickly pulled into the front yard; Bodie and Will were just coming out of the barn heading back to the doublewide. Will ran back into the barn and out the back.

"Send one of the dogs after him and check the barn." called Sgt. Woods.

The dog ran Will down in under a minute. He held him there until one of the handlers showed up and cuffed him. In the barn, they found Brad.

"The investigator is in the barn," yelled one of the team, "tied up but not hurt."

"OK, get him out and into one of the cars," said Sgt. Woods.

Bodie had run into the doublewide.

"Not very smart," Sgt. Woods said to Sheriff Hodges. "Essentially he ran into a jail."

Using a bullhorn, the Sheriff called out. "OK Bodie, time to come out. You're surrounded. We're going to take you in dead or alive and I really don't care which."

"Keep your cover." Sgt. Woods told his team, "We don't know what he has in there."

"What do you think, Sarge?" said Sheriff Hodges.

Woods told one of his men to get Will over to him. Now he asked him "Do yourself some good here, Varilly. Cooperate with us and we'll put it in the report. What weapons you got in the house?"

"I got a shotgun and a 30.06 rifle, that's all," said Will "but Bodie has one of those kick ass pistols, a .357 magnum. He has it with him. I saw it when he got here."

"Okay." said Sgt Woods, then to one of the team, "Put him back in the car and stay with him. I don't want any brother hero stuff."

The sergeant got on the bull-horn and called, "What's it going to be Bodie, decision time. You're not getting out of here. It's over"

Bodie wasn't talking but they knew he was in there. They saw movement through the curtained front window.

"No sense to have a big shoot up and risk my guys getting hurt." said Woods to the Sheriff. "We know he's in there and ain't going nowhere. Let's fill the trailer with tear gas and see what happens. If that doesn't work, we can throw in a couple of flash bangs and give him one hell of a headache."

Woods got three of his men to position themselves so they could launch the gas canisters through the large living room window as well as the kitchen and bathroom windows. One canister would have been adequate for the size of the trailer but Woods wanted him out quickly.

"I want to take him alive if we can," Woods said, "but if you're at risk, take him down. Three of you guys put on masks in case we have to go in. Now, on my command."

When the command came to fire, three tear gas canisters hit the trailer almost simultaneously. It didn't take long for the whole trailer to be engulfed in thick smoke. Bodie might have lasted 15 seconds, not much more. He came crashing out of the front door, his .357 firing wildly. He was almost blind from the gas and could barely stand up.

"Hold all fire" yelled Sgt. Woods.

Blinded, Varilly didn't see one of the techs run at him from the side and bring his weapon down on his wrist. Bodie dropped the gun. After that, he put up no resistance. He was desperate to get a breath of clean air. The effect of the gas on him was dramatic. He could barely see and began vomiting uncontrollably.

"Cuff him and put him in one of the cars after he stops puking," said Sgt. Woods.

"Nice job, Sergeant," said Sheriff Hodges. "You and your guys are a great team."

Chapter 21

DURING THE INTERROGATIONS Will confessed they planned to put Brad in the trunk of the car and drop them both into the gravel quarry. Bodie had also talked about putting him on a plane.

"What plane," asked Sheriff Hodges.

"Bodie has a plane with a load coming in tonight. It drops off a load and then heads back to Tennessee," said Will. "Happens about two times a month. Sometimes drops off drugs and goes back and other times drops a load and goes on."

"What time?" asked Sheriff Hodges

"We never know," said Will. "Around midnight but it can be two hours either side, they land, text us at the trailer, and then we go out there."

"But one is coming in tonight?" asked the Sheriff.

"That's what Bodie told me," said Will.

The Sheriff called Sgt. Woods back in and told him "I need you and your guys again tonight. There is a drug plane coming into the Varilly farm."

"What? There's a landing strip there?" said Sgt. Woods

"Sure is. Brad found it today," said the Sheriff. "You can't easily see it from the road and it's not obvious unless you're right there. Brad recognized it from his flying days."

Sgt Woods briefed his team about the arrival of the drug plane.

"We'll check the wind direction so we know which end of the landing strip to be on. We want to be in position when it finishes its landing roll out. Stay under cover and when it stops, shoot out the tires and engines if you can get a good bead on them. I don't want any shots at the cockpit, we'll want to talk to these intrepid aviators."

Sheriff Hodges went back into the interrogation room and asked Will, "Are there any special signals or communications with these guys ahead of the drop?"

'No," said Will. "Like I told you before, we stay in the trailer and they send a text telling us they're there. We drive out and pick up the stash".

"Just making sure." said the Sheriff. "What kind of stuff do they bring in?"

"Mostly cheap grade heroin from Mexico and cocaine from who knows where in South America," said Will. Now that he was cooperating he couldn't tell them enough. "We sell some locally but most of it goes to Albany, Rochester and Buffalo. Bodie handles all that. I don't know nothing about it."

"Does any money change hands?" asked the Sheriff.

"Yeah" said Will, " Bodie gives them a bag of cash every time."

"How much?" asked the Sheriff.

"I don't know the amounts, but a lot. Bodie deals with it. You'll have to ask him."

"So why do you live in this shithole and Bodie in a scrappy house in Binghamton?" asked the Sheriff.

"We wanted to lie low. We were going to roll the operation up soon and live happily ever after." said Will.

"Where did you keep the money? On the farm?" asked the Sheriff?

"May as well tell you. You will find it anyway," said Will. "In the old horse stalls. Two chest freezers buried in each stall. ten stalls, twenty freezers."

"All loaded with cash?" asked the Sheriff.

"Pretty much. All in hundreds and fifties and packed tight. A couple of million in each freezer I guess."

"Shit bang." said the Sheriff. "All off the backs of dumb ass middle class yuppies and desperate people who got hooked on the stuff. Why didn't you bail out before? You got more money than God, what were you going to do with it?"

"Bodie was never satisfied." said Will, "Just one more freezer, one more freezer, it never ended. I really thought about emptying one and just disappearing. Wish I had."

"The supplier never would have let you," said the Sheriff. "You try to bail out, you'd be a dead man. It was always gonna be 'you lose' ... either way. They would never let either of you out."

And with that sobering reflection, Sheriff Hodges left Will Varilly to his own thoughts.

"Okay then," he said to the Swat Team, "let's go meet the incoming flight! There's probably drinks in the Arrivals Lounge."

Chapter 22

THERE WAS A GOOD COVERAGE of woods around the air strip, so they could conceal themselves quite easily. Around 1AM after they had been in place for three hours, they heard the sounds of a twin-engine plane north of the landing strip. It was circling almost as if it was waiting for a landing clearance. After about 15-minutes it established itself on a long final approach. These guys were very careful even though they probably had done this many times before. This was the kind of landing strip you need to know well to get in safely, especially at night. Margins are thin and you don't want to make any mistakes.

The twin engine plane was a Beech Baron, no longer in production but a great workhorse. Solid and with great low speed handling characteristics.

When the plane landed it did a full rollout on the runway to the south and started to turn so it could get to the other end of the runway to be ready for departure. As it was turning on the runway, Sgt. Woods called the command to open fire and the tires were shot out, both main landing gear and nose wheel. They were not going anywhere. One of his snipers put a few bullets into the left engine just to make sure. Sgt. Woods kept his men in place and out of sight. The pilots had nowhere to go, they were trapped.

"Okay guys, time to come out," Woods called out on the bullhorn. "Or we shoot up the plane with you inside. One at a time with your hands up. Leave any weapons in the plane."

Nothing happened for maybe two minutes. Maybe they were evaluating their options, but he didn't want to give them time to make contact with their people. He gave the order for one of the sharpshooters to put a few bullets into the nose of the aircraft. Not hit the crew but letting them know about the firepower on the ground. Three bursts of gunfire to the front of the aircraft did the trick. Two pilots came out, hands held high. They were quickly cuffed and put in one of the cars, under guard.

The plane was loaded with drugs. No rear seats, just piles of drugs. Maybe 500 lbs. What's that in kilos wondered the Sheriff. Kilos were the metrics of the drug trade. He had his team inventoried the drugs and money and took them to the station. They had taken this about as far as they could. Next step was to bring in DEA and the State Police.

Sheriff Hodges called the DEA and at first they didn't believe his story. How could a county hick sheriff break a huge operation like that? After he proposed going to the newspapers, they quickly came around and sent a team to Tompkins county to "manage" the ongoing investigation. The evidence at the Sheriff's office was impressive. Nearly 250 kilos of drugs, over a million in cash and the usual drug runners' weapons, semi-automatic rifles, and UZIs known in the trade as street sweepers. And that wasn't counting the money in the freezers.

The pilots were turned over to the DEA. However, Sheriff Hodges, insisted on keeping Bodie for the attempted murder charge against Brad and the murder of Jake Hagan. He didn't care about Will and let DEA have him. He was a talker and might be of interest to them.

Bodie tried to talk his way into a deal but Sheriff Hodges told him, "We don't need you Bodie, your cousin can't stop talking and the pilots will give the DEA their route network. The DEA has what they want and we have what we want - you! You ain't got nothing to sell".

Chapter 23

BRAD CALLED LULU THAT night to tell her he had to stay in Tomkins county with Sheriff Hodges to finish up the paperwork on the case. He didn't go into much detail about the events, other than to say he was fine. He knew he had to tell her everything, but felt it better to do it in person. But he would have to be quick as this was a major national news story and the media would be all over it.

When Brad got back to Binghamton the next day, he checked in with Spud and Mary Louise on his way home.

"Brad, I am so sorry," said Mary Louise. "I never thought this case had so many moving parts. We really put you at risk. Please forgive us. We just didn't imagine anything like this."

"I didn't know either," Brad said. "At the end it just opened up into a bottomless pit. I never would have pegged the Varillys as big-time drug dealers. When the Sheriff recovered the money from the stables, it was over $18,000,000. Sure beats farming I guess."

"By the way," Mary Louise said. "Phil Raimondi arrested Linda Hagan as an accessory to the murder. She helped Bodie conceal evidence after he killed Jake. So, she'll face some serious jail time also."

"What about the kids?" asked Brad.

"Maybe a bright spot there." said Mary Louise. "Her sister and family are solid and have a great relationship with the kids. They'll foster them and by the time Linda gets out of prison, they'll be young adults. By then, the kids will be able to make their own decisions regarding the future with their mother. In the meantime, they're in a very good place, Spud will tie up the case. We'll take it in front of a grand jury and then to trial. It's pretty much a slam dunk with Will and Linda's confessions and

Bodie has no chance now that the Toyota has been tied to him. He's finished also."

"So," Brad said, "case closed."

"Yes," said Mary Lou "and again many thanks. I never imagined it would put you in such a high-risk situation. I hope this doesn't mean you will never do any more work for us."

"Let's see what comes along, answered Brad. " Maybe we just need to be careful on the field work part of it!"

"I hate to bother you with this now," said Spud, as he walked his friend out of the DA's office. "but I still have some family issues that need your attention, Brad."

"I know and I have a way forward," but I need to meet with all of you to get the ball rolling. It is a family matter and can only be a family solution," replied Brad.

"I'll do whatever it takes," said Spud.

"I need a couple of days to decompress and spend some time with LuLu. Me not coming home the other night really worried her. I need to explain it all in detail and calm her concerns. This was not your average part time gig!"

Chapter 24

THE FOLLOWING WEEK, Brad met with Spud, Erin and Jaime at their house.

Brad started out, "I'm not sure how much you know about mediation other than the name, so let me explain the process. In a mediation, all decisions are made by the parties. That means it's you who all make the decisions, not the mediators. We help facilitate the conversation but do not make any recommendations on a way forward. We do not function as therapists, lawyers, clergy or judges. It's an informal process not a court proceeding. To put it simply, you drive the bus. If you want to do this, I can schedule a mediation at the Resolution Center. You'll do a brief intake with one of our case managers who will get the usual contact information from you. After that, a mediation session is scheduled with you. A session typically lasts two hours. We find that after two hours; the parties need to step back. We can always schedule another session if required. If you do reach a satisfactory resolution on the issues in play, we write a memorandum covering the agreement so the parties have a game book for the future. Questions?"

Jaime asked "Can you be our mediator?"

"I could," said Brad, "but I know you all and to maintain objectivity it is better to have mediators unknown to you. One of the risks in a mediation process is that one or both of the mediators could "tilt" towards one of the parties. If that happens the decisions of the parties can be influenced and that is not desirable. By the way, complete confidentiality is important to us and your case will not be discussed, even with me."

"Can we talk with you after the mediation?" asked Jaime.

"Sure you can," said Brad, "and you may find that, as time goes by, you'll want to modify the memorandum. Nothing is cast in concrete. It's a living document. OK?"

Two weeks later, Spud's family found themselves at The Resolution Center meeting with Ross and Judy, two of the more experienced mediators. They started the session by asking Jaime what his thoughts were on the current situation and what he wanted to see changed. Finding out what was really bothering Jaime was important to addressing the issue. It actually took two sessions to get it all on the table and when they did the solutions were not draconian.

It turned out Jaime was very worried about the relationship between his parents and what was going to happen in the future. It took some time for them to establish a level of trust where Jaime felt that whatever happened, he was loved and would always be a part of their lives. To start with, he was scared and angry. He had reasoned that if he behaved badly, they would be afraid to get divorced and they would get back together. Erin had been very worried about his behavior and had been overly strict in trying to keep it under control. Spud had felt as if he was in the middle of a storm and did not know what to do.

Spud and Erin did not initially understand why Jaime had behaved the way he had, but once they did see it, a way forward started to emerge. Surprisingly, it was Jaime who broke the code. He asked them if they would go to a marriage counselor. There was an excellent service in town called The Samaritan Counseling Center. Erin had heard about it from LuLu who had been on the Board at the center for a number of years. Spud initially felt it would be embarrassing to talk about their issues in public, so to say. But he overcame his male reluctance and agreed. The mediators told Jaime that the marriage counselor might even want to meet with him at some point. That was not a problem for him as by then he was completely invested in the process. Erin called the center and set up the initial appointment.

When they finished the mediation process, Ross and Judy helped them write a memorandum detailing the agreement between them and reviewed their wording with them. Then they signed it. This was an emotional commitment for the parties, perhaps most of all for Jaime. The memo was quite simple. Jaime recognized that his parents may not come back together but regardless he was and would remain part of the family. To this end, he would try to do better at school and change his lifestyle habits. Spud and Erin would go to a marriage counselor and sort their relationship issues. They would meet periodically as a family and see how things were going. Jaime was happy with the outcome and renamed the memo "The Rules of Engagement!" Spud and Erin were pleased as well, as they had been dodging the issue of their relationship for too long and clearly it had taken a toll on the family.

Chapter 25

BRAD AND LULU SAW SPUD, Erin and Jaime socially over the next few months but did not discuss how things were going. It appeared that things were on the mend. Then Brad and LuLu went to England to visit Lulu's mother and were away for two months. When they returned and met with their friends, things had improved dramatically. Spud announced that he and Erin were thinking about getting back together. They were taking it slowly. When asked about the future, they said "we shall see" and laughed.

Jaime had a strong school year and played AAU basketball for the Southern Tier Storm in the summer league. He said it was hard as he was the youngest player on the team and the older guys were really good. But he was getting good playing time and told Brad that he was working on his fade away jump shot.

Jaime had also made contact with Linda's son Gary who was in foster care with his aunt and family, not very far away. They played a lot of pick-up basketball and Gary was always at Jaime's AAU games. Darlene did not totally understand what had happened and it would take time to work through it all. Dad was dead, Mom was in jail. It was a lot for the children to deal with in their lives. Initially, they felt that it was their fault and they had caused the marriage breakup and the death of their father. The child therapist had taken them through this and slowly they were beginning to have a base to build on for the future. They say kids are resilient. Don't believe it, thought Brad. Like all of us it takes time and help to understand the events and then address them. But he was hopeful. They had great support from their aunt and uncle. Spud, Erin and Jaime were now a major part of the children's lives also. With time and support, hopefully, they would understand it all.

"Well," said Brad to himself, "this had been quite a year." He'd solved a murder and helped break up a major drug ring though he'd damn near got killed in the process. His golf hadn't improved much, but he'd helped a family get back on track. He had more work with the DA to look forward to, and the Resolution Center was always after him to do mediations. He was in a good place.

The End

IF YOU ENJOYED THIS first Upstate Mystery, please leave a review. They are REALLY important for new Authors!

Website https://upstatemystery.com

I have four new novellas in the Upstate Mystery series with familiar characters that you met in *Hit and Run*.
https://books2read.com/ap/8pyqGA/fj-donohue

Closure: An abduction of a child thirty years ago was never solved. It has always haunted Coach McCarthy. An accidental discovery brings it all back.

Closure
An Upstate Mystery
FJ Donohue

RIGHT TIME WRONG PLACE: A murder in an assisted living home. Who would want to kill this defenseless lady? Elton Hendricks, a transfer from the NYPD who with the help of familiar local characters, discovers the truth.

THE CARIBBEAN LAUNDRY: An independent accountant is murdered in his home. Detective Elton Hendricks investigates and a lucky find opens up a crime far beyond this quiet upstate town

TWO MURDERS BY THE River: Two homicides within minutes of each other! Robbery? Revenge killing? Contract hit? The police have to solve this quickly, or the impact of this horrific crime on the town will be devastating.

Detectives Hendricks and Adams embark on an investigation that takes them far outside of upstate New York to another country.

Nobody will feel safe until the crime is solved

About the Author

If you enjoyed this novella, please leave a review.

You can contact me at frankjd3@gmail.com

I'M A RETIRED INTERNATIONAL Sales Director, having worked in the commercial and military flight simulation industry for over 30 years. I lived in Brussels (Belgium) and Bonn (Germany) for eight years and met my British wife in Brussels. Before my career in the flight simulation industry, I was an Armament and Electronics Maintenance Officer in the USAF. We have three children and seven grandchildren. Since retirement I continue to chase an ever-elusive golf game.

Home is a small town in central New York State where the novellas are set.

I'm a volunteer mediator and Lemon Law arbitrator. In the novellas I always have one of the characters involved in a mediation or a Lemon Law claim.

This is my first novella and I plan on releasing a series of Brad Petronella cozy mysteries. If you would like to email me (address above) I'll let you know when the next one comes out. I won't use your information for any other purpose.

An underlying theme in my novellas is people helping people. In spite of the difficulties and crime that may surround us, there is always hope in friendship and good neighbors.

Don't miss out!

Visit the website below and you can sign up to receive emails whenever fj donohue publishes a new book. There's no charge and no obligation.

https://books2read.com/r/B-A-CFSO-DZYOB

BOOKS2READ

Connecting independent readers to independent writers.